THE TRUE
CROSS

BRIAN WILDSMITH

OXFORD   LONDON   MELBOURNE

OXFORD UNIVERSITY PRESS
1977

The first man God created was Adam.
God gave him a beautiful garden to live in,
called Eden. The garden was watched over by
an Angel. To keep Adam company God created
Eve. Adam and Eve loved and cherished each
other and were happy. But the time came when
they disobeyed God. He had forbidden them to
eat the fruit of the Tree of the Knowledge of
Good and Evil. But Adam and Eve were
tempted, and did so.

Because of their disobedience, God punished
Adam and Eve by banishing them from Eden.

So the Angel drove them out of the garden of Eden,
saying to Adam:

"Before you die, I will send you a gift which will bring forgiveness to you and your children."

Adam and Eve had many children, and lived to be very old. As Adam was dying he remembered the Angel's words, and sent his son Seth back to the Garden of Eden. The Angel gave Seth a sprig from another tree in the Garden, the Tree of Life, and told him to plant it in Adam's mouth after his death.

Adam died,
so Seth planted the sprig
in his father's mouth.

The sprig grew into a
magnificent tree.
Animals and birds found shelter
among its enormous branches
and roots.

One day a blind man, exhausted by the heat of the day, took shelter in the shade of the tree and fell asleep. On waking he found to his astonishment that he could see. Overcome with joy he ran to tell others of the miracle.

Before long many sick people came to the tree to be miraculously healed.

Rapidly the tree's fame spread.

Centuries passed, and men forgot about the tree's powers. It was cut down and its timber was used to build a bridge over a stream called Siloam, near Jerusalem.

However, when the fabled Queen of Sheba visited King Solomon, she came to the bridge and realising that it was built from the Tree of Life, knelt down and worshipped the wood.

"For this sacred wood" she said, "all the earth will tremble and sun and moon grow dark and the veil within the temple be rent from top to bottom."

Her prophesy eventually
came true.
When Jesus of Nazareth
was condemned to death
a cross was made for him
from the wood of the
bridge over Siloam.

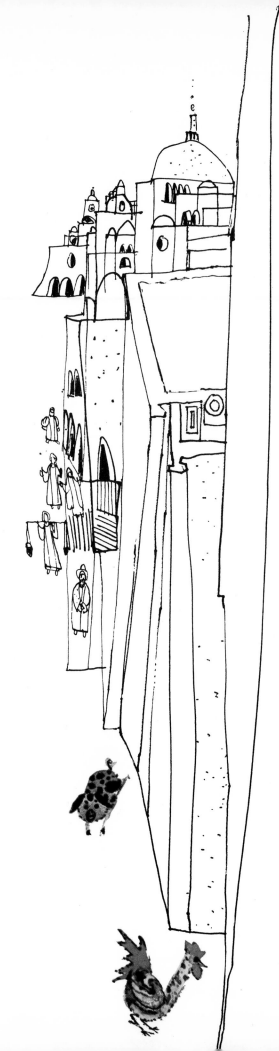

Carrying his cross, Jesus was led from Jerusalem to a hill called Calvary, where he was crucified between two thieves.

The earth trembled and darkness covered the whole land.

After Jesus' death, his cross and those of the two thieves were buried in the earth.

Over two hundred years later the tyrant Maxentius and his army were preparing to invade the City of Rome, which was ruled by the Emperor Constantine.

The night before the attack Constantine had a dream.

He saw a cross shining in the sky.
So when he awoke he had a replica of it made for him.
Holding it in outstretched hands he walked towards
Maxentius' army, which on seeing it fled in fear.

This miracle convinced Constantine of the truth of the Christian faith. His mother Helena also became a Christian and devoted herself to the task of finding the True Cross.

After many years of searching she came across a man called Judas, who indeed knew where the cross could be found. But he refused to reveal his secret. Helena, therefore, had him thrown into a dry well for six days without food. Only on the seventh day did Judas agree to tell her.

He led Helena to the hill of Calvary where the cross had been buried, together with those on which the two thieves had died.

A temple had been built where the crosses had
been buried, so Helena had this pulled down.
Judas himself led the digging, and eventually they
found the three crosses, but they could not
distinguish the True Cross from the others.

So the body of a young man who had died that day in Jerusalem was brought up to Calvary, and each cross in turn was laid over him. When the True Cross touched him he came alive again. It still retained the power from the Tree of Life.

Oxford University Press, Walton Street, Oxford OX2 6DP

Oxford London Glasgow New York Toronto Melbourne Wellington Cape Town Ibadan Nairobi Dar Es Salaam
Lusaka Addis Ababa Kuala Lumpur Singapore Jakarta Hong Kong Tokyo Delhi Bombay Calcutta Madras Karachi

© Brian Wildsmith, 1977

ISBN 0 19 279718 2

All rights reserved. No part of this publication may be reproduced, stored in a retrieval system,
or transmitted, in any form or by any means, electronic, mechanical, photocopying, recording or otherwise,
without the prior permission of Oxford University Press.

Printed in Great Britain by W. S. Cowell Ltd., Ipswich